Note to parents, carers and teachers

Read it yourself is a series of modern stories, favourite characters and traditional tales written in a simple way for children who are learning to read. The books can be read independently or as part of a guided reading session.

Each book is carefully structured to include many high-frequency words vital for first reading. The sentences on each page are supported closely by pictures to help with understanding, and to offer lively details to talk about.

The books are graded into four levels that progressively introduce wider vocabulary and longer stories as a reader's ability and confidence grows.

Ideas for use

- Ask how your child would like to approach reading at this stage. Would he prefer to hear you read the story first, or would he like to read the story to you and see how he gets on?

- Help him to sound out any words he does not know.

- Developing readers can be concentrating so hard on the words that they sometimes don't fully grasp the meaning of what they're reading. Answering the puzzle questions at the end of the book will help with understanding.

For more information and advice on Read it yourself and book banding, visit www.ladybird.com/readityourself

Book Band 8

Level 3 is ideal for children who are developing reading confidence and stamina, and who are eager to read longer stories with a wider vocabulary.

Special features:

Detailed pictures for added interest and discussion

Wider vocabulary, reinforced through repetition

Bomb wasn't at the slingshot. But the birds did find something there. "Look!" said Red. "It's one of Bomb's! He must have been here!"

12

13

Longer sentences

Simple story structure

Red told the Blues about some of the birthday parties Bomb had had before. They had all ended the same way – with a very big bang!

22

23

Educational Consultant: Geraldine Taylor
Book Banding Consultant: Kate Ruttle

A catalogue record for this book is available from the British Library

This edition published by Ladybird Books Ltd 2014
80 Strand, London, WC2R 0RL
A Penguin Company

001

ISBN: 978-0-72328-901-2

Printed in China

BOMB'S
BEST BIRTHDAY

Written by Richard Dungworth
Illustrated by Jorge Santillan

It was a new day on Piggy Island –
and not just any old day.
"Hooray!" said Chuck. "It's
Bomb's birthday!"

The birds were all very excited.
"We'll have a big party for him!"
said Matilda. "With a cake!"
"We'll have to find him first," said
Red. "Do you know where he is?"

9

They looked all over for Bomb.
"Where has he gone?" asked Matilda.
"What about the slingshot?" said
Chuck. "We haven't looked there."

Bomb wasn't at the slingshot. But the birds did find something there. "Look!" said Red. "It's one of Bomb's! He must have been here!"

Red was right. Bomb had been at the slingshot – before the others got up. He had used it to fly off to a mountain top, some way away.

Right now, Bomb was all alone on the mountain, feeling sad. This wasn't how he wanted to spend his birthday. But he believed it was the best thing to do.

Back at the slingshot, the little Blues were feeling sad, too. "Why would Bomb fly off?" they asked Red. "Doesn't he like having a party?"

"Bomb loves having a party!" said Red. "That's just it. He likes his birthday so much, he gets too excited. And we all know what happens then!"

Red told the Blues about some of
the birthday parties Bomb had had
before. They had all ended the same
way – with a very big bang!

"He doesn't want to blow up," said Red, "but he can't help it. And when he does, it isn't safe for us – or for the eggs!"

"He must have gone away so that he doesn't do any harm," said Matilda sadly. "But he can't spend his birthday alone!"

"I've got it!" said Red. "If Bomb can't come to his party, we'll just have to take his party to him! Here's what we'll do…"

A cake was part of Red's plan. Matilda hurried off to make it. It would be a cake like only she could make.

The other birds did as Red told them. They all had a part to play in his plan. Chuck was just as excited as the Blues.

On the mountain, Bomb was feeling very down. What if he did his best not to get over-excited? No, it was no good.

"This is the only safe way," he thought

"Well done, Matilda!" said Red,
as she hurried back with her cake.
"Now – into the slingshot, all of you!
It's time to fly to the target!"

Bomb was looking sadly down
from the mountain, when a call
from above made him look up.
He couldn't believe what he saw.

"Hooray for Bomb!" called Red. "Happy Birthday!" called the others. Then Matilda dropped the cake – right on target!

Bomb loved the cake. He loved his birthday flyover, too. He may have been sad before, but now he was feeling very happy.

He was feeling so happy now that there was only one thing for it.

After all, who could he harm way up here...?

How much do you remember about the story of Angry Birds: Bomb's Best Birthday? Answer these questions and find out!

- Whose birthday is it?

- Where does Bomb go by himself?

- What has happened at Bomb's other birthday parties?

- Who makes Bomb a cake?

- How do the other birds cheer Bomb up?

- What does Bomb do at the end?

Look at the different story sentences and match them to the characters who said them.

"Why would Bomb fly off?"

"What about the slingshot?
We haven't looked there."

"We'll have a big party for him!
With a cake!"

"This is the only safe way."

Read it yourself with Ladybird

Tick the books you've read!

For more confident readers who can read simple stories with help.

Level 3

- ☐ YOU won't like this present as much as I DO!
- ☐ The Elves and the Shoemaker
- ☐ Hansel and Gretel
- ☐ Harry and the Bucketful of Dinosaurs
- ☐ Jack and the Beanstalk
- ☐ The Red Knight
- ☐ Fury on Music Island
- ☐ Poppet Stows Away
- ☐ Rapunzel
- ☐ Aladdin
- ☐ The Jungle Book
- ☐ Roxy and the Great Escape
- ☐ Angry Birds: Chuck
- ☐ Angry Birds: Bomb's Best Birthday

Longer stories for more independent, fluent readers.

Level 4

- ☐ I am Inventing an Invention
- ☐ Harry and the Dinosaurs United
- ☐ Heidi
- ☐ Katsuma and the Art Thief
- ☐ Luvli and the Glump-a-tron
- ☐ The Pied Piper of Hamelin
- ☐ Sam and the Robots
- ☐ Snow White and the Seven Dwarfs
- ☐ The Wizard of Oz
- ☐ The Little Mermaid
- ☐ Alice in Wonderland
- ☐ Oddie The Hero
- ☐ Angry Birds: Red and the Great Fling-off
- ☐ Angry Birds